Robinson Crusoe

Artists: Penko Gelev
Sotir Gelev

First edition for North America (including Canada and Mexico), Philippine Islands, and Puerto Rico published in 2011 by Barron's Educational Series, Inc.

All inquiries should be addressed to:
Barron's Educational Series, Inc.
250 Wireless Boulevard
Hauppauge, New York 11788
www.barronseduc.com

ISBN-13 (Hardcover): 978-0-7641-6303-6
ISBN-10 (Hardcover): 0-7641-6303-5
ISBN-13 (Paperback): 978-0-7641-4451-6
ISBN-10 (Paperback): 0-7641-4451-0

Library of Congress Control No.: 2010929888

Picture credits:
p. 40 Topham Picturepoint © 1999/Topfoto.co.uk
p. 44 Mark Bergin

Every effort has been made to trace copyright holders. The Salariya Book Company apologizes
for any omissions and would be pleased, in such cases, to add an acknowledgment in future editions.

Date of Manufacture: January 2011
Manufactured by: Leo Paper Products, Ltd., Heshan, Guangdong, China

Printed and bound in China.
Printed on paper from sustainable sources.
9 8 7 6 5 4 3 2 1

Robinson Crusoe

Daniel Defoe

Illustrated by

Penko Gelev

BARRON'S

Retold by

Ian Graham

Series created and designed by

David Salariya

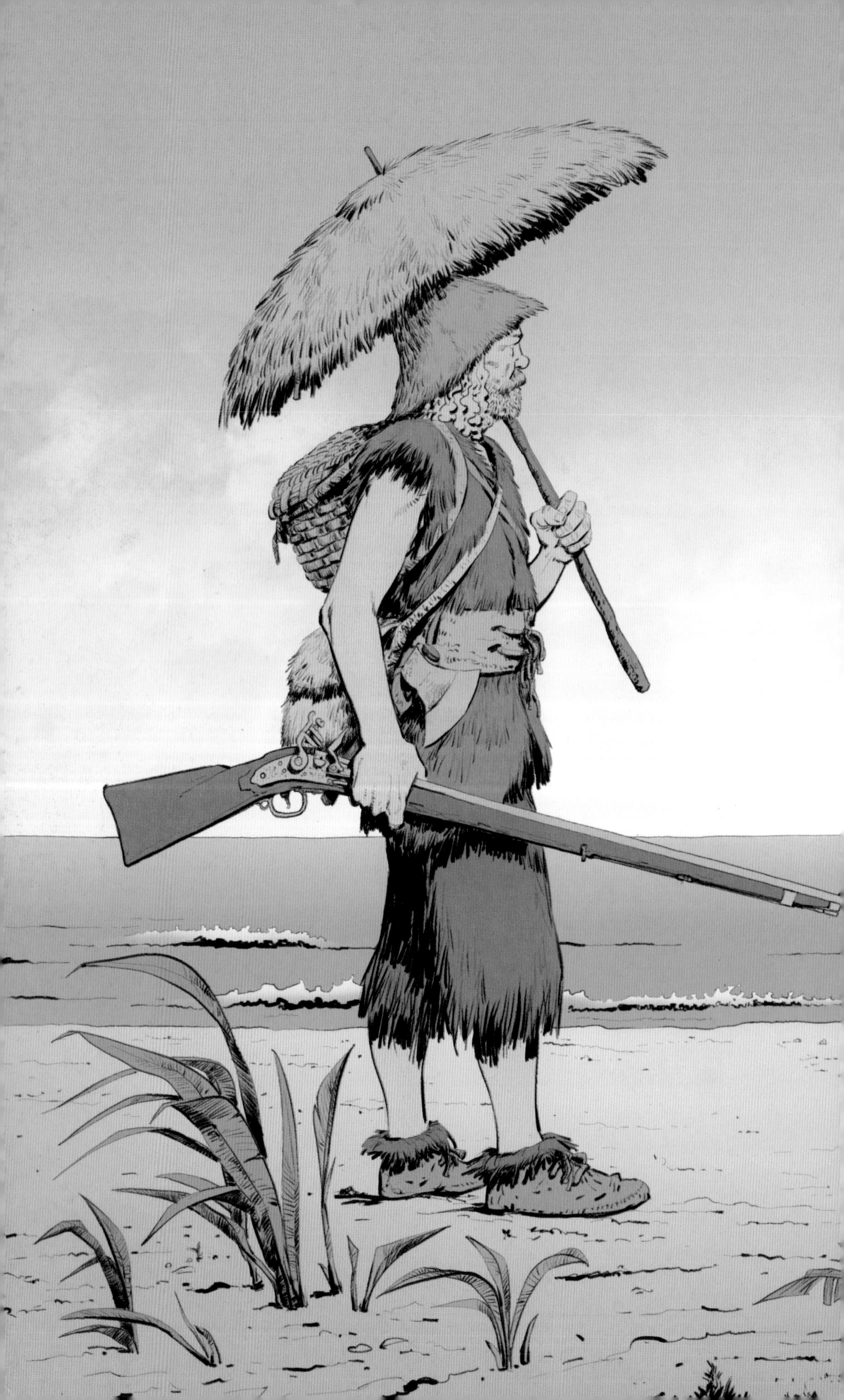

I am divided
from mankind —
a solitaire;
one banished from human society.

But I am not starved,
and perishing on a barren place,
affording no sustenance.

CHARACTERS

Robinson's mother

Robinson's father

Robinson Crusoe

Xury, a slave of the
pirate captain

Friday

A plantation owner
in Brazil

A Moroccan
pirate captain

THE CALL OF THE SEA

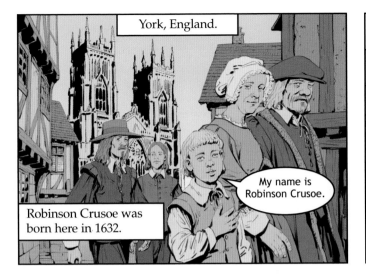

York, England.

Robinson Crusoe was born here in 1632.

My name is Robinson Crusoe.

His oldest brother, a soldier, died fighting the Spanish.

Nobody knows what became of his second brother.

Robinson's father wants his son to be a lawyer, but Robinson has other ideas.

I will be satisfied with nothing but going to sea!

His father asks him why he is so determined to leave home.

What reasons more than a mere wandering inclination[1] do you have for leaving your father's house?

When his father becomes upset, Robinson at first agrees to stay at home…

My heart is so full[2] I can say no more.

…but his dream will not leave him.

He tells his mother that his mind is made up.

I am resolved[3] to run away and see the world.

1. a mere wandering inclination: a careless wish to travel.
2. My heart is so full: I am experiencing such strong feelings (in this case, sadness).
3. I am resolved: I have decided.

LEAVING HOME

Robinson meets a friend while visiting the port of Hull.

I'm going by sea to London in my father's ship.

He has finally got his chance to go to sea!

September 1, 1651.

Robinson Crusoe boards a ship for the first time.

As the wind tosses the ship about, he becomes terribly seasick and fears for his life.

Please, God, if you will spare my life on this one voyage, I will go directly home.

His friend teases him.

You were frighted[1] when it blew a capful of wind.[2]

Feeling better, he forgets his vow to return home.

The ship is soon forced to shelter from another storm.

Strike the topmasts![3]

The wind increases. Even the captain fears for their fate.

Lord be merciful to us! We shall all be lost![4]

---

1. frighted: frightened. 2. a capful of wind: a light breeze. 3. Strike the topmasts: Lower the top section of each mast (to reduce the ship's wind resistance). 4. We shall all be lost: We will all die.

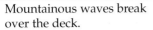

Mountainous waves break over the deck.

The crew cut down the masts to save the ship.

She's going to founder![1]

Lord save us!

We have sprung a leak.

There is four foot[2] of water in the hold.[3]

The captain orders guns to be fired to signal for help.

BOOM!!

FIRE!

A boat arrives just in time.

She's sinking!

Just 15 minutes later, they see their ship disappear beneath the waves.

I should be laughed at were I to return to my home in such a miserable state.

My thanks to you for such great humanity.[4]

Robinson and the other sailors are given food and lodging by their rescuers.

Robinson decides that he can't go home a failure, so he must move on to London and go back to sea.

1. founder: sink.   2. foot: feet.
3. hold: the part of a ship where the cargo is stored.   4. humanity: kindness.

VOYAGE INTO SLAVERY

In London, a ship's captain invites Robinson on his next voyage to Africa. Robinson jumps at the chance.

If you would go the voyage with me as my messmate[1] and companion...

...there will be no expense.

The captain schools Robinson in the art of navigation.[2]

The heat near the equator[3] gives Robinson a fever.

But he proves to be a successful trader, returning to London a wealthy man.

Now I am a sailor *and* set up as a Guinea[4] trader.

The captain falls ill during the voyage and dies soon after his return to England.

Farewell, friend.

Ashes to ashes, dust to dust...[5]

The new commander of the captain's ship invites Robinson to return to Africa with him.

Shall we voyage together?

Aye, sir.

Will you keep this safe for me?

Robinson leaves most of his fortune with the captain's widow for safekeeping.

Off the coast of West Africa...

I see a Sallee rover![6]

...a pirate ship looms out of a gray morning.

1. messmate: someone to share meals with on a ship.
2. navigation: planning a course to reach a destination.
3. equator: an imaginary line around the middle of the Earth.

4. Guinea: a common name for Africa in the 17th century; nowadays, Guinea is a republic in western Africa.   5. Ashes . . . dust: part of the funeral service in the *Book of Common Prayer.*   6. Sallee rover: a pirate ship from the port of Salé in Morocco.

Robinson and the rest of the crew lie in wait for the pirates.

The guns thunder, sending cannonballs smashing into the pirate ship.

FIRE!

Fight for your lives!

Sixty pirates board the ship and start slashing the sails and rigging.[1]

Enough! With three men killed and eight wounded, we are obliged to yield.[2]

The crew have no chance of winning, so they surrender.

Robinson and the crew are taken as slaves to the Moroccan port of Salé.

You shall be my proper[3] prize, my slave.

The pirate captain claims Robinson as his personal slave.

My father was right — he said I should be miserable, with none to relieve[4] me, if I went to sea.

He is put to work cleaning the pirate captain's house.

1. rigging: the ropes and chains that hold up a ship's masts and control the sails.
2. obliged to yield: forced to surrender.   3. my proper: my own.   4. relieve: rescue.

A Chance at Freedom

After two years, the pirate captain starts taking Robinson fishing with him.

Ready the pinnace![1]

One day the captain sends Robinson fishing without him.

A Moor[2] called Ishmael and a slave called Xury go with him.

Robinson secretly loads extra supplies.

He tricks Ishmael into bringing gunpowder and lead shot.[3]

I shall bring powder and shot.

We may shoot some alcamies.[4]

They sail a mile offshore and start fishing.

Robinson suddenly grabs Ishmael around the waist…

Aarrgghh!

…and tosses him into the sea.

I beg you, take me into the boat. Don't leave me here to drown.

You swim well enough to reach the shore.

If you will be faithful to me, I'll make you a great man.

Xury is afraid he might be thrown overboard too, but Robinson trusts him.

---

1. pinnace: a small boat with sails and oars for travelling between a ship and the shore.   2. Moor: a Muslim from North Africa.   3. lead shot: pellets used as ammunition.   4. alcamies: small brown shore birds with long, curved bills.

After five days' sailing, they anchor in the mouth of a river.

The night is full of animal noises from the forest.

Let us weigh anchor[1] and row away.

No!

BLAM!

Robinson fires into the water to frighten off a beast they hear approaching the boat.

In the morning they wade ashore.

Robinson keeps watch while Xury searches for drinking water.

We will eat well tonight.

Xury shoots a hare-like animal for dinner.

They find fresh drinking water further upstream.

Dreadful monsters!

They sail along the coast, looking for an English ship that might take them home.

1. weigh anchor: raise the anchor.

RESCUE

Robinson recognizes a group of islands and immediately knows where he is.

Those are the Cape de Verd Islands.[1]

Xury spots a ship and fears it might be the pirate captain coming to recapture them.

Master, master, a ship with a sail!

They are in luck; it's a Portuguese merchant ship.

A sailor on the ship spots their tiny boat in the distance.

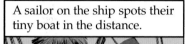

They've seen us. They're shortening sail.[2]

It is some European boat!

The sailors question Robinson in various languages.

¿Quiénes sois?

Qui êtes-vous?

What are you?

I am an Englishman fleeing from slavery under the Moors in Sallee.

You may take everything I have in return for my deliverance.[3]

No, Seignor Inglese,[4] I will carry you thither in charity.[5]

The ship's captain refuses any payment for saving Robinson and taking him to Brazil.

When they arrive in Brazil, Xury decides to stay with the ship and work for the captain.

1. Cape de Verd Islands: the Cape Verde Islands, off the west coast of Africa.   2. shortening sail: furling (rolling up) some of their sails to make the ship slow down.   3. deliverance: rescue.   4. Seignor Inglese: Mister Englishman.
5. I will carry you thither in charity: I will take you there free of charge.

14

Robinson sells the captain a leopard skin and a lion skin.

He stays with the owner of a sugar plantation[1] and learns about the sugar business.

He buys some land and sets up his own plantation.

I live like a man cast away upon some desolate[2] island.

He feels lonely, working so hard that he rarely sees anyone else.

...and then the ship was struck by a monstrous wave.

At the port of St. Salvadore[3] he amazes the merchants with his adventures.

Will you sail with our ship and bring back workers for our plantations?

Three merchants are sending a ship to Africa to buy slaves.[4]

Robinson accepts the offer. He makes a will[5] in case he does not return.

September 1, 1659.

Eight years to the day after he left his parents, Robinson boards another ship.

We will use these beads, shells, and other trifles[6] for trading.

1. plantation: a large farm or estate where crops are grown to be sold.   2. desolate: bleak.   3. St. Salvadore: now called Salvador da Bahia. It was the capital of colonial Brazil from 1549 to 1763.   4. slaves: Buying people in Africa to work as slaves in the Americas was common at this time; the slave trade was not banned until the 19th century.   5. will: a legal document setting out what is to happen to a person's money and possessions after his or her death.   6. trifles: worthless things.

SHIPWRECK!

At first the sea is calm and the weather is extremely hot.

Man overboard!

A terrible storm overwhelms the ship. One sailor is washed into the sea.

We should go directly back to Brazil.

No, we should make for the Carib-Islands.[1]

After the storm, Robinson persuades the captain to set course for the Caribbean.

But a second storm drives the ship westward, away from the Caribbean.

Land ahoy!

In the morning, the lookout spots land.

The ship hits a sandbar,[2] sending the crew flying.

There is no hope for the ship. The crew must take their chances in a small boat.

They row for the shore, fearing their boat will be smashed to pieces.

A mountainous wave tips the boat over and the sailors spill out.

1. Carib-Islands: the islands of the Caribbean Sea.
2. sandbar: a long, narrow sandbank.

Dragged under the waves, Robinson gasps for breath.

A wave carries him onto the sand…

…but before he can get away to safety, an even bigger wave pulls him back into the sea.

I can't believe it. My life is saved.

Robinson finally drags himself up the beach and out of danger.

Is there not one soul saved but myself?

There is no sign of the crew.

How is it possible that I could reach the shore alive?

Ah, sweet water!

He manages to find some fresh water to drink.

Fearing that he might be eaten by animals while he sleeps, he spends the night in a tree.

SCAVENGING[1] SUPPLIES

By morning, the storm has calmed.

The ship is sitting upright on rocks near the shore.

Robinson swims out to see what he can salvage.[2]

He finds food in the ship's bread room.

I have need of a raft.

He builds a raft to carry supplies back from the ship.

This should keep me fed awhile.

He finds three seamen's chests and fills them with food.

This fits me well.

He looks for clothes – the ones he left on the beach have been washed away.

Steady as she goes.

The rising tide and an onshore breeze help him back to the shore. The ship's dog swims ashore with him.

1. scavenging: stripping something discarded in order to reuse its material.   2. salvage: save from the wreckage.

The tide carries the raft up a creek.

Robinson finds a flat piece of ground to land the raft on.

He climbs a hill to get a better view of the land.

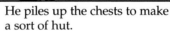

He piles up the chests to make a sort of hut.

There is time to make one more trip to the ship before nightfall.

He builds a second raft and loads it with more supplies.

Then he builds a shelter to cover anything that would be ruined by rain or sun.

The supplies he finds on the ship include money – which is utterly useless to him now!

1. What art thou good for?: What use are you?

MOVING HOME

Robinson realizes he will need a more secure home.

He finds the perfect place –

– a natural hollow at the foot of a rock.

He marks out the front wall of his new home.

He builds a strong wall by driving stakes into the ground.

He takes apart his old camp and moves the supplies to his new home.

To make his home secure, he enters and leaves by a ladder, not a door.

He pitches a tent on the plain and covers it with a tarpaulin.[1]

He hacks rock out of the hollow to make a small cave.

1. tarpaulin: a heavyweight waterproof cloth, made of tarred canvas in Robinson's time.

Fearing his gunpowder might be struck by lighting and explode, he divides it into small parcels and keeps them in different places. He uses his guns to hunt goats.

Oh, my powder!

I shall enjoy a dinner of the finest goat meat!

He starts a calendar by cutting notches on a post.

In time, he builds a more permanent wooden roof for his home.

Although unskilled in carpentry, he makes a table and chair for himself.

He starts keeping a diary.

He makes a lamp from a clay dish full of goat fat with some rope fibers as a wick.

EARTHQUAKE!

"What is this? Barley . . . and rice!"

Robinson finds crops growing where he had emptied a bag of chicken feed.

Suddenly...

"The ground beneath my feet trembles!"

A violent earthquake strikes his island.

Rock falls from the roof of his cave and tumbles down the hill above it.

"The powder is ruined by water."

He finds a barrel of gunpowder washed up on the beach.

After a storm, pieces of the wreck of his ship are washed up further along the shore.

"Everything I can get from her will be of some use to me."

He spends more than a month cutting up the wreck and dragging the wood away.

"I shall dine on turtle tonight!"

He catches a turtle to eat.

"Turtle meat is most savory and pleasant."

It's a welcome change after eating only goats and birds.

"I shall surely die for want of help."

The next day he is seized by a fever. His body is racked by shivering, sweating, and violent headaches.

The fever lasts ten days.

I shall ne'er[1] be short of fruit.

Recovered, he explores the island and discovers a fertile valley. Melons and grapevines grow in abundance.

He spends the night sleeping in a tree.

Such lush and verdant[2] growth!

The next day he discovers cocoa trees, then orange, lemon, and lime trees.

A mightily wholesome[3] and refreshing drink.

He makes himself a fruit drink…

…and then returns with bags to collect more fruit.

These should furnish my self[4] for the wet season.

I shall dry these grapes to make raisins.

This will serve as my country house!

He builds himself a bower[5] in the valley.

Rain, rain, and more rain.

Shall I ever leave this place?

He shelters in his cave during the rainy season. It rains nearly every day from August to October.

The notches on his calendar show he has been on the island exactly a year.

1. ne'er: never.   2. verdant: green.   3. wholesome: healthy. An illness called scurvy was common among sailors at this time. It was later found to be due to a shortage of vitamin C, and was treated by adding citrus fruit (oranges, lemons, limes, etc.) to the diet.
4. furnish my self: provide for me.   5. bower: a woodland shelter made of branches.

Farmer Crusoe

After the rains, Robinson sows barley and rice.

But his seeds fail to grow, because the soil has already dried out.

He sows more seeds in February, knowing that the rain will water them in March and April.

He tries his hand at making baskets.

Exploring more of his island, he sees land in the distance.

This side of the island is covered with grassland, woods, and flowers.

He decides to keep a parrot as a pet.

On the seashore he finds turtles, animals running around, and birds in the trees.

After his exploration he returns home for a well-earned rest.

I have now been three years in solitary confinement.[1]

What with hunting and cooking, time passes quickly.

Robinson builds a fence to stop animals eating his crops.

I shall hang them for a terror to the others.[2]

He shoots several birds and hangs them over his land to scare the other birds away.

He makes a scythe[3] from a cutlass[4] to harvest his crops.

He sows all his seeds on a new, bigger plot of land.

He teaches his parrot to say its name – the first word he has heard spoken in more than three years.

Poll! Poll!

He digs clay to make pots…

I see I have another problem to set my mind to.

…but the big ones crack as they dry out.

This piece is hard as stone — an agreeable accident.[5]

One piece of pottery falls into his cooking fire and is hardened by the heat.

Now he hardens and strengthens his clay pots by building a fire around them.

1. in solitary confinement: entirely alone (the phrase usually refers to imprisonment).   2. for a terror to the others: to frighten the other birds.   3. scythe: a hand tool with a curved blade to cut grass or grain crops.   4. cutlass: a short, broad slashing sword commonly used by sailors at this time.   5. agreeable accident: an unexpected outcome that is acceptable.

A Near-Disaster

Robinson thinks about escaping from the island. He tries to turn the ship's boat the right way up, but it is too heavy to move.

He resolves to build a new boat by hollowing out a tree trunk.

It takes five months of hard work – and then he realizes that he can't move it down to the water. It's too heavy!

The clothes he saved from the ship are worn out.

He makes a new suit of clothes from goat skins.

A goatskin umbrella keeps off the rain and the sun.

He builds a smaller, lighter boat and digs a channel to get it to the creek.

Success at last!

1. periagua: a dugout canoe.

He adds a mast, and a sail made from pieces of sail salvaged from the ship.

Now he sets out to sail around his island.

He plans to stay close to shore, because his new boat is too small to venture into the open sea.

But a strong current takes him out to sea!

Eventually the wind changes and delivers him, exhausted, back to the shore.

In the morning he continues around the coast, looking for a creek to let him sail inland.

He finds a convenient harbor for his boat and sets off on foot for home.

He rests at his shelter in the fertile valley.

He wakes from a deep sleep to hear his name being called, as if in a dream – but it's only Poll, the parrot.

1. amply victualled: well supplied with food.
2. whither: where to?

A FOOTPRINT

With little powder left, Robinson's guns will soon be useless for hunting.

…but they easily bite through his snares.[1]

Next, he digs deep pits to trap them.

He covers the pits with hurdles[2] and scatters food.

In the morning, he finds three kids – a male and two females – in one of his traps.

He has to drag them to their new home in the valley.

He tames the goats by feeding them from his hand.

He fences in part of the meadow to keep the goats in.

After two years he has a flock of 43 goats, which provide all the meat and milk he needs.

1. snares: traps.   2. hurdles: panels made of thin, twiggy branches woven together.

What stares would I draw,[1] were I to travel through Yorkshire as I am?

He wonders what his fellow countrymen would make of him if they saw him dressed in his animal skins.

How can this be?

One morning he makes an astonishing discovery.

He dashes back to his cave, terrified that he might be attacked at any moment.

Such noises as I never heard before!

He lies awake all night. His imagination runs away with him. Ordinary noises fill him with dread.

He convinces himself that he must have made the footprint himself – but when he compares it to his foot, the footprint is much bigger.

The footprint is not mine!

I must erase all signs of my presence from the land.

He decides to destroy his crops, animal pens, and fences to hide his existence.

No, I will hide myself from the eyes of visitors.

In the morning he changes his mind; he will just take care not to be seen by anyone.

I will be safe as if in a fortress.

He fortifies his home by building a strong outer wall and setting up his muskets[2] ready to be fired through it at any attackers.

1. What stares would I draw?: What strange looks would people give me?
2. muskets: guns with a long barrel, fired from the shoulder.

CANNIBALS!

Horror!

I must show a fierce bearing[2] to my enemies.

The smoke from my fire could give me away.

One day, Robinson makes a grisly discovery on the beach. His island has been visited by cannibals![1]

He tries to look as tough, fearsome, and well-armed as possible, to scare off anyone thinking of attacking him.

This will fit my purpose.

Be this a devil or a man?

…but he is not alone!

Returning with a torch, he finds that the eyes belong to a goat too ill even to stand up.

Frighted by a sick he-goat!

He finds a big cave where he can light a fire safely…

The next day, he moves supplies into his new cave.

My visitors are returned.

Early one morning, he spots the light of a fire on the shore. The natives are making regular visits to the island.

1. cannibals: people who eat human flesh.
2. a fierce bearing: a frightening appearance.

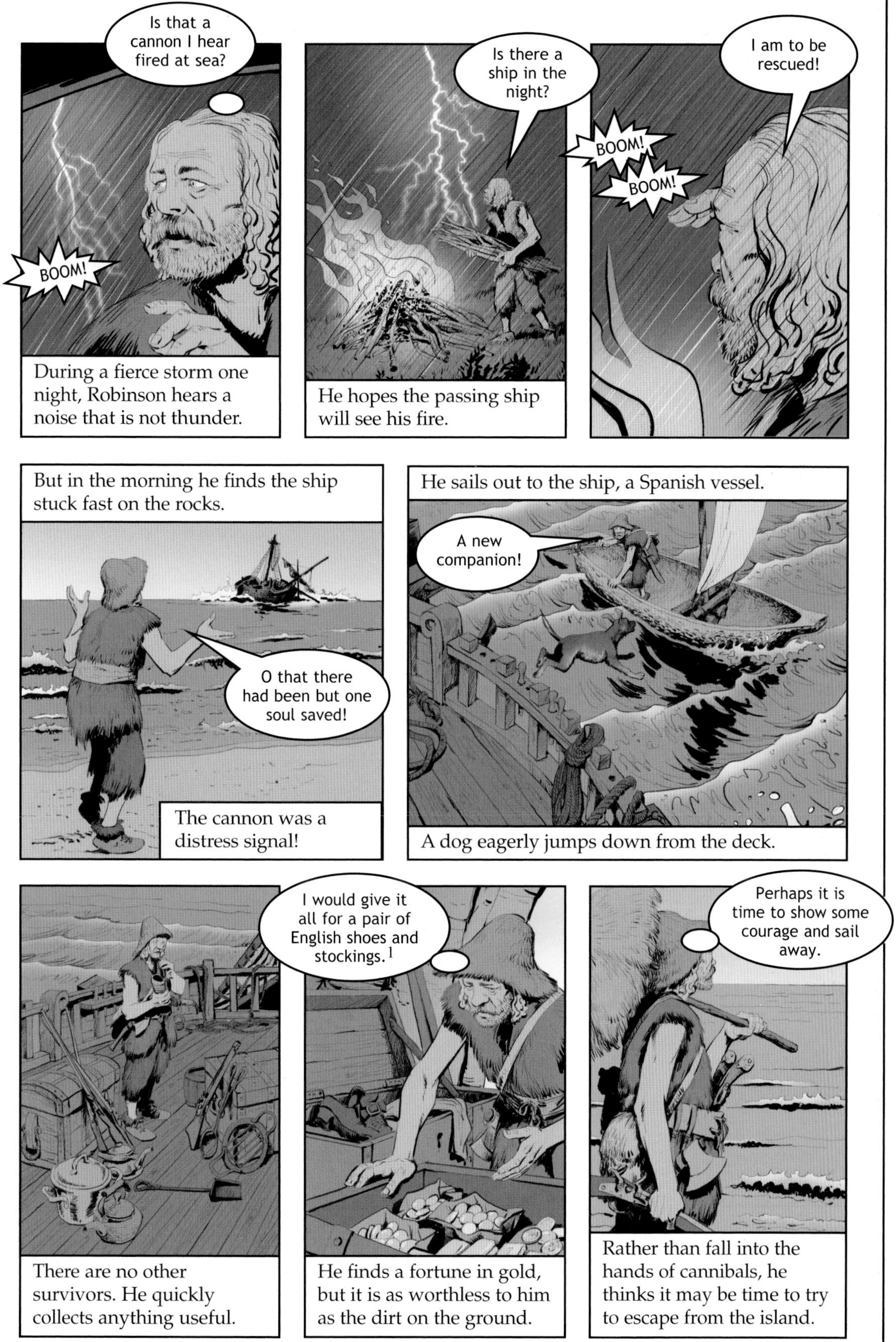
Is that a cannon I hear fired at sea?
BOOM!
During a fierce storm one night, Robinson hears a noise that is not thunder.
Is there a ship in the night?
He hopes the passing ship will see his fire.
BOOM!
BOOM!
I am to be rescued!
But in the morning he finds the ship stuck fast on the rocks.
O that there had been but one soul saved!
The cannon was a distress signal!
He sails out to the ship, a Spanish vessel.
A new companion!
A dog eagerly jumps down from the deck.
There are no other survivors. He quickly collects anything useful.
I would give it all for a pair of English shoes and stockings.[1]
He finds a fortune in gold, but it is as worthless to him as the dirt on the ground.
Perhaps it is time to show some courage and sail away.
Rather than fall into the hands of cannibals, he thinks it may be time to try to escape from the island.

1. stockings: socks.

Friday

One morning, Robinson discovers 30 natives on the beach – far too many for him to fight off if they see him.

They have two prisoners. One breaks free.

The prisoner swims across a creek, followed by two of his captors.

As the prisoner runs past, Robinson steps out and knocks the first native to the ground with the stock of his gun.

What a strange custom!

The second native aims an arrow at Robinson, who shoots him dead.

The prisoner shows his gratitude to Robinson for saving his life.

As the first native comes to, the prisoner kills him with Robinson's sword.

The prisoner quickly buries the bodies so they will not be found.

Robinson gives the prisoner food and water in his cooking cave.

He names the prisoner after the day when he saved him.

You Friday. Me Master.[1]

You are almost as well clothed as your Master.

Friday, this is where you will sleep.

Robinson gives Friday new clothes and makes a place for him to sleep.

BANG!

Friday is terrified by the noise of Robinson's gun.

Robinson later sees Friday talking to the gun.

I believe he would worship it!

He is begging it not to kill him.

Robinson teaches Friday to speak English.

He shows him how to farm the land and look after the animals.

1. Friday, Master: Crusoe, a European, assumes that he is superior to other races. This attitude was usual at the time when the story was written. Instead of asking what Friday's real name is (which is of no interest to Robinson), he gives him a new English name.

A New Boat

Friday, are your people's canoes often lost at sea?

No, canoes go with current in the morning and come home with current in afternoon.

Robinson quizzes Friday about his people's travels on the ocean.

I know where we are!

Robinson realizes that Friday is talking about tides washing in and out of the great Orinoco River.[1]

There, beyond the moon,[2] white-beard mans like you.

Can we go to these men?

Yes, yes, in two canoe.[3]

This is the boat that brought me here.

Me see such boat at my nation.

Friday thinks they can reach the place where the white-bearded men live.

Robinson shows Friday the remains of the ship's boat.

We save the white mans from drown in boat like this.

They must be from the ship cast away[4] in sight of my island.

Friday, do you wish yourself in your own nation?

I be much glad to be at my own nation.

Such a boat carry much vittle.[5]

But the wood is split and rotten.

But your boat too small.

Friday, I have a bigger boat.

Robinson remembers the bigger boat he built years earlier – but it is in a poor state now.

1. Orinoco River: one of the longest rivers in South America, in present-day Venezuela and Colombia.
2. beyond the moon: in the west, where the moon sets.   3. two canoe: a large boat the size of two canoes.
4. cast away: wrecked.   5. vittle: victuals (food and other provisions).

Friday thinks he has done something wrong and is being sent away.

Why you angry mad with Friday? Why send Friday home?

No, no, Friday, I go too.

They start building a new boat.

This tree make good periagua.

It takes them a month to finish their new boat, and two weeks to push and drag it to the water.

She floats!

Robinson teaches Friday how to sail the boat.

This stout roof will keep the rain off our boat.

They build a small dock to store the boat in until the weather is fair enough for them to leave.

An English Ship

Friday, see if you can find us a turtle on the seashore.

At the end of the rainy season, Robinson and Friday lay in supplies for their voyage.

Friday spots a ship anchored near the island.

Master, they are come!

An English ship!

Eight sailors bring three prisoners ashore in a longboat.[1]

While the guards sleep, the prisoners are shocked to see a wild, fur-clad man creeping up to them.

Gentlemen, do not be surprised at me.

I am the ship's commander. My crew has mutinied.[2]

Let us retreat out of their hearing, lest they awake.

If I venture upon your deliverance,[3] will you carry me and my man[4] to England?

Here are three muskets for you, with powder and ball.[5]

Robinson offers to help the captain if he will take him and Friday to England. The captain agrees.

Robinson arms the prisoners with guns from his store.

1. longboat: an open boat with oars and a sail, carried aboard a ship.   2. mutinied: taken control of the ship and made the captain their prisoner.   3. If I venture upon your deliverance: If I take the risk of rescuing you.
4. my man: my servant.   5. powder and ball: gunpowder and lead bullets.

The leaders of the mutiny must not be allowed to escape.

The mutineers wake to find the captain almost upon them.

Rouse yourselves!

Swear your allegiance to me[1] and I will spare your miserable lives.

Another longboat is sent ashore to see what has happened.

They have firearms with them.

When the new arrivals call out to their companions, Friday answers them.

Hollow![2]

Hollow!

He leads the mutineers all over the island following the sound of his voice.

Hollow! Hollow!

This is truly a land of demons and spirits.

The exhausted men surrender, believing that the island is haunted.

The captain and some of his crew row out to the ship and board it.

BLAM!

When the mutineer leader is shot dead, the captain is once again in command of his ship.

1. Swear your allegiance to me: Promise to follow my orders.   2. Hollow: Hello.

COMING HOME

The captain gives Robinson a suit of English clothes. They feel very strange!

Two of the mutineers decide to stay on the island rather than face execution.

Stay here and keep your lives, or leave with us in irons and go to the gallows.[1]

Robinson keeps his goatskin cap, his umbrella, and one of his parrots.

December 19, 1686.

Finally, I am bound for England!

Robinson leaves the island behind after 28 years, 2 months, and 19 days.[2]

I am as perfect a stranger to all the world as if I had never been known here.

Back in England, everything has changed. His friends have all gone.

You owe me nothing.[3]

The captain's widow has fallen on hard times. He helps her all he can.

In York, he learns that his parents are dead, but finds two sisters and two nephews.

He travels to Lisbon in Portugal, for news of his plantation in Brazil.[4]

Your plantation has prospered.

Can this really all be mine?

Robinson's partner in Brazil sends him the profit from his plantation.

---

38 1. go to the gallows: be hanged for mutiny.   2. 28 years, 2 months, and 19 days: Robinson's arithmetic is wrong! He was shipwrecked on September 30, 1659 (see his calendar sign on page 21), so he has been there 27 years, 2 months, and 19 days. 3. You owe me nothing: You need not return the money you were keeping for me.   4. Portugal, Brazil: Brazil was a Portuguese colony at this time; it became independent in 1822.

Robinson is so dazed by the news of his new wealth that a doctor has to be called.

The patient will recover with a little bloodletting.[1]

He has a fortune of more than £5,000 in coin and a large estate in Brazil.

It seems I am a rich man.

Robinson sets off for England on horseback with Friday and a group of other travellers.

In the Pyrenees,[2] Friday sees snow for the first time and is afraid of it.

What is this that makes my skin hurt?

It's called snow.

Their guide is attacked by wolves. Friday shoots one of the wolves, which scares the others away.

O Master! O Master!

A bear walks out of the wood onto the path. Friday taunts it fearlessly before killing it.

You fool, he will eat you up!

Me shakee te hand with him! Me makee you good laugh.

On English soil again, Robinson sells his Brazilian estate for a fortune.

What an uncommon adventure I have had!

1. bloodletting: slitting open a vein to let blood trickle out. In earlier centuries this was believed to be a cure for many different illnesses. 2. Pyrenees: a range of mountains on the border between Spain and France.

The End

DANIEL DEFOE (c.1660–1731)

Daniel Defoe was born in London in about the year 1660. The exact date of his birth is unknown. His name at birth was Daniel Foe, and his parents were Alice and James Foe. His father was a tallow chandler – a maker and seller of candles made from tallow (fat obtained from sheep and cattle). Both his parents were dissenters (Christians who had broken away from the Church of England), and young Daniel was brought up as a dissenter. He considered becoming a clergyman, but went into business instead. By 1683 he had become a general merchant, selling hosiery, woollen goods, tobacco, and wine. He travelled extensively throughout England and Europe in the course of his business.

In 1684 Foe married Mary Tuffley. On his marriage, he received a dowry of £3,700. (A dowry is a gift of money or goods given to a husband by his wife's family.) Daniel and Mary had eight children, six of whom survived.

The year after they were married, Foe joined the Monmouth Rebellion, an attempt to overthrow the newly crowned King James II. The rebellion failed and most of its participants were executed or transported to the Americas; Foe was lucky to escape punishment.

MONEY WORRIES
In 1692 Foe was arrested because of unpaid debts, which may have been as high as £17,000 (worth more than half a million dollars today), and declared bankruptcy. After a series of different jobs, he set up a brick and tile factory in Tilbury, Essex. Around 1695 he started

An engraved portrait of Daniel Defoe, based on a painting by Jeremiah Taverner.

calling himself De Foe, which later became Defoe. Two years later, he wrote *An Essay on Projects*, which proposed a variety of social and economic reforms for banks, insurance societies, asylums, roads, and schools.

In the early 1700s he turned his attention to politics and religion. It wasn't long before his views landed him in trouble. In 1703 he was arrested for writing an inflammatory pamphlet called *The Shortest Way with the Dissenters*. He was sentenced to stand in the pillory, a wooden frame in which a man's head and arms were locked. After three days in the pillory he was sent to London's Newgate Prison. While he was in prison, his factory went out of business and he was bankrupt again.

After six months, he received a pardon thanks to Robert Harley, the Speaker of the House of Commons. In return for his release, Defoe agreed to work as a spy for Harley. At the same time, he was also writing political news sheets and pamphlets.

THE GREAT STORM

In 1704 Defoe wrote his first book, called *The Storm*. It was a collection of first-hand accounts of a real storm, known as the Great Storm of 1703. This is reputed to be the worst storm ever to hit the British Isles. Wind speeds are thought to have exceeded 118 mph. About 8,000 sailors died as their ships were wrecked and sunk in the North Sea. On land, whole rows of houses were levelled, 400 windmills were destroyed, a million trees were blown over, and many churches lost their spires and towers.

In the same year, Defoe started writing *The Review*, a paper that was published three times a week. Its contents included news and essays on government policy and trade, and articles on manners and morals. Defoe wrote all of it himself.

ROBINSON CRUSOE

In 1713 and 1714 Defoe was arrested on several occasions because of his political writings and further unpaid debts. In 1719 his most famous book was published. Now known simply as *Robinson Crusoe*, its full title was:

The Life and Strange Surprizing Adventures of Robinson Crusoe, of York, Mariner: Who lived Eight and Twenty Years, all alone in an un-inhabited Island on the coast of America, near the Mouth of the Great River of Oroonoque; Having been cast on Shore by Shipwreck, where-in all the Men perished but himself. With An Account how he was at last as strangely deliver'd by Pyrates. Written by Himself.

Defoe continued to publish successful novels, including *Memoirs of a Cavalier*, *Colonel Jack*, *Moll Flanders*, and *The Life, Adventures and Piracies of the Famous Captain Singleton*. He also wrote travel books, including *A Voyage Round the World* and *A Tour Thro' the Whole Island of Great Britain*. And he wrote books on personal conduct and behavior, including *The Family Instructor* and *The Compleat English Gentleman*. He even wrote about ghosts, including *An Essay on the History and Reality of Apparitions*. *A Journal of the Plague Year* is a history of the Great Plague of 1665, written as though it were an eyewitness account.

LASTING MYSTERIES

By 1724 Defoe was quite wealthy again. He had a large house with stables and grounds built for himself at Stoke Newington, London. He appears to have had property elsewhere, too. But by the time of his death, on April 24, 1731, he was once again suffering from money trouble. He died at lodgings in Ropemaker's Alley in Moorfields, London, and was buried at Bunhill Fields. No one knows how he lost his wealth, or why he did not die at home.

PIRATES

Daniel Defoe's life almost exactly spanned a period of history known as the Golden Age of Piracy. Acts of robbery and violence against ships have probably existed since the beginning of sea travel, but our idea of what pirates looked like and what they did dates from Defoe's time.

European countries, mainly England, France, the Netherlands, Portugal, and Spain, established colonies in the New World (the Americas) and the Far East from the 15th century onward. As their empires grew, seaborne trade across the Atlantic Ocean increased, and so did piracy. Pirates patrolled the busy sea routes, picking off ships and stealing their valuable cargoes.

LEGAL PIRATES

There were two types of pirates. Privateers were authorized by their government to attack enemy ships. The government took a share of any treasure the privateers seized, and the privateers grew rich on the rest. For the government, it was an inexpensive way to wage war on its enemies.

But pirates proper had no government backing. They attacked whoever and wherever they wished and kept all the proceeds. They were hunted by the navies of the colonial powers and, if caught, could expect to be executed.

Pirate ships were unusually democratic for the time. The captain and quartermaster of a pirate ship were elected by the crew. They then appointed the rest of the officers. When treasure was seized in battle, it was shared among the crew – though the captain and officers received bigger shares than the rest of the crew. Some of the money was kept back and saved in a fund that was used to pay compensation to injured crewmen.

THREE OUTBREAKS

There were three outbreaks of piracy during the Golden Age. The first began around 1650 and lasted about 30 years. It was caused by conflict between England, France, and Spain over their colonies in the Caribbean and Central America. The pirates preyed on ships carrying captured treasure, mainly gold and silver, from the New World to Europe.

The second outbreak of piracy lasted from 1693 to the end of the century. During this period the pirates left the Caribbean, where there were fewer valuable cargoes and ports to attack, and focused on the Indian Ocean instead. This period was known as the Pirate Round after the route the pirates sailed. From the Caribbean, they sailed around the southern tip of Africa into the Indian Ocean. Then, after a stop at Madagascar for supplies, they carried on to attack valuable shipping on the sea routes between the Red Sea and India. Then they returned to the Caribbean to sell their booty.

The Pirate Round came to an end in 1700. In 1697 a base on Madagascar, where pirates resupplied their ships, was lost when its owner, Adam Baldridge, was driven out by local people. In addition, the Indian Ocean shipping was increasingly being protected by heavily armed warships, so there were not such easy pickings anymore. Finally, the War of the Spanish

Succession had broken out in Europe, offering pirates more opportunities for privateering closer to home.

The final phase of the Golden Age of Piracy began when the War of the Spanish Succession ended in 1714. Thousands of sailors and privateers found they were no longer needed, and many of them turned to piracy. In 1715 a fleet of 12 galleons carrying treasure to Spain sank in a hurricane off Florida. Salvage ships were immediately sent to the area with divers to recover the valuable cargoes. Pirates soon heard about the treasure and raided the salvage operation. They made off with the treasure and set up a base in the Bahamas. From there, they attacked shipping in the Caribbean and along the American coast.

The pirate threat was so serious that merchant ships travelled in convoys protected by warships. European countries, tired of having their merchant ships attacked, built up their navies to meet the pirate threat. Bases used by the pirates were destroyed and their ships were hunted down. By about 1720, the Golden Age of Piracy had ended.

NOTORIOUS PIRATES OF THE GOLDEN AGE

Henry Morgan	c.1635–1688	Became Lieutenant Governor of Jamaica.
Bartholomew Roberts	1682–1722	The most successful pirate of the Golden Age; captured more than 470 ships.
Edward Teach ("Blackbeard")	c.1680–1718	Went into battle with smoking fuses sticking out from under his hat.
Anne Bonny	c.1698–1782	One of very few female pirates.
Henry Every	1653–c.1699	One of the few pirates who retired without being arrested or killed in battle.
Jack Rackham ("Calico Jack")	1682–1720	Named after his colorful clothes, made of calico (coarse cotton fabric).
William "Captain" Kidd	c.1645–1701	Rumored to have left buried treasure which has never been found.
Thomas Tew	d.1695	Pioneered the route known as the Pirate Round.
William Dampier	1651–1715	The first pirate to sail into the Pacific Ocean, and the first person to circumnavigate the world three times.

ALEXANDER SELKIRK
THE REAL ROBINSON CRUSOE?

The story of Robinson Crusoe was probably inspired by the real-life adventures of Alexander Selkirk. Selkirk was born in Scotland in 1676. He ran away to sea in 1695 to avoid appearing before the Kirk Session (church court), charged with bad behavior in church.

At sea, he proved to be a skilled navigator. In 1703 he joined a ship called *Cinque Ports*, a 16-gun privateer, on an expedition led by William Dampier (see page 43). British privateers mainly attacked Spanish ships off the coast of South America.

MAROONED

By 1704, Selkirk was so worried about the seaworthiness of the *Cinque Ports* that he feared it might sink. He asked to be put ashore at the next stop. His wish was granted when the ship stopped to take on water at the Juan Fernández Islands. The islands, then uninhabited, are about 414 miles from the coast of Chile in the Pacific Ocean. Selkirk set up home on an island called Más a Tierra (which means "closer to land" in Spanish).

When his clothes wore out, he made new clothes from goat skins. After several years, he was delighted to see two ships anchor off the coast of his island, but they turned out to be Spanish. When some of the crew came ashore, they shot at Selkirk. He hid until they left again.

Alexander Selkirk wonders whether he made the right decision.

RESCUED

On February 1, 1709, just over four years after Selkirk was marooned on Más a Tierra, two English ships arrived and he was rescued. He discovered that he had been right to leave the *Cinque Ports*; it had sunk off the coast of Peru, with the loss of most of the crew. He resumed his career as a privateer and returned to Scotland a wealthy man in 1712. In 1713 an account of his adventures was published. Six years later, Daniel Defoe wrote *Robinson Crusoe*.

Selkirk was unable to settle on land. He joined the Royal Navy and became a lieutenant on the Royal Naval vessel *Weymouth*. Aboard the *Weymouth* he died of a fever, probably yellow fever, off the coast of Africa on December 13, 1721. He was buried at sea.

RECOGNITION

In 1966 the Chilean government changed the name of one of the Juan Fernández Islands, Más Afuera ("further off"), to Alejandro Selkirk and renamed Más a Tierra, the island where Selkirk actually lived, Robinson Crusoe.

c.1660
Daniel Foe (later Defoe) is born, probably in Cripplegate, London.

1660
Charles II is restored to the English throne, having been exiled during the English Civil War and Commonwealth period.

1665
The Great Plague sweeps through London, killing 15 percent of the population.

1666
The Great Fire of London destroys 80 percent of England's capital city.

1676
Alexander Selkirk is born in Lower Largo, a village in Fife, Scotland.

1683
Foe becomes a general merchant.

1684
Foe marries Mary Tuffley.

1685
James II becomes king of England. Foe joins the unsuccessful Monmouth Rebellion.

1688
James II flees from England during the so-called Glorious Revolution.

1689
William III and Mary II become king and queen of England.

1692
Foe is declared bankrupt and imprisoned.

1694
Foe establishes a brick and tile factory in Tilbury, Essex.

1695
Foe starts calling himself De Foe, which becomes Defoe. Alexander Selkirk runs away to sea.

1697
Defoe's first book, *An Essay on Projects*, proposes radical reforms.

1702
William III dies and Queen Anne becomes the last monarch of the House of Stuart.

1703
Defoe is imprisoned for his pamphlet *The Shortest Way with the Dissenters*. His factory goes out of business and he is bankrupt again. Speaker Robert Harley arranges his release.

1704
Defoe writes *The Storm*, based on the real-life Great Storm of 1703.

1704
Alexander Selkirk is marooned on a deserted island, Más a Tierra, in the Juan Fernández group off the coast of Chile.

1707
England and Scotland are united to become the Kingdom of Great Britain.

1709
Selkirk is rescued by an English privateer ship, the *Duke*.

1713
Defoe is arrested because of his political writings and unpaid debts. An account of Selkirk's adventures is published.

1718
The notorious pirate Edward Teach, also known as Blackbeard, is found and killed.

1719
Defoe publishes *The Life and Strange Surprizing Adventures of Robinson Crusoe, of York, Mariner* and *The Farther Adventures of Robinson Crusoe*.

1720
The infamous pirate John Rackham, known as Calico Jack, is executed. Defoe's novel *The Life, Adventures and Piracies of the Famous Captain Singleton* is published.

1721
Alexander Selkirk dies while serving with the Royal Navy off the coast of Africa.

1722
Defoe's novels *Colonel Jack*, *Moll Flanders*, and *A Journal of the Plague Year* are published.

1731
Defoe dies on April 24 and is buried in the dissenters' cemetery at Bunhill Fields, Finsbury, London.

1732
Defoe's widow, Mary, dies.

*R*obinson Crusoe was first performed on stage in 1781. It was presented as a pantomime at London's Drury Lane Theatre by the famous playwright Richard Brinsley Sheridan. In this, Crusoe and Friday rescue a band of comic players from cannibals. In 1867 French composer Jacques Offenbach wrote a comic opera based on Sheridan's pantomime.

Later pantomime versions added new characters to make the story more entertaining: a native princess, King Neptune, and Robinson Crusoe's girlfriend, Polly Perkins. Sometimes there is a villain called Will Atkins or a pirate called Blackbeard for the audience to boo and hiss at. Other versions include Robinson's mother and his brother Billy.

Robinson Crusoe was performed on stage up to the 1980s. By then the racial, colonial, cannibal, and slavery elements of the original story made it a difficult subject for popular entertainment.

ON SCREEN

More than 50 versions have been made for the cinema and television. The first film was made in 1913. A 1954 film starred Dan O'Herlihy, who was nominated for an Oscar. A 1997 version starred James Bond actor Pierce Brosnan.

Some filmmakers have tried to update the traditional story. In 1964, *Robinson Crusoe on Mars* told the story of an astronaut stranded on the Red Planet. In *Swiss Family Robinson* (1960), based on an 1812 novel by Johann David Wyss, the Robinson family is shipwrecked on a desert island. Dick van Dyke starred in a film called *Lt. Robin Crusoe, U.S.N.* in 1966. He plays a U.S. Navy pilot who bails out of his plane and ends up on a desert island. There he is joined by a chimpanzee that took part in the U.S. space program, and a native girl called Wednesday.

The 1975 film *Man Friday* tells the traditional story in a new way. Crusoe (Peter O'Toole) discovers Friday (Richard Roundtree) and sets out to change him from a "savage" (as Crusoe sees him) into a civilized man. But as the story unfolds, Friday turns out to be far wiser than Crusoe.

One of the most popular small-screen versions was a French series called *Les Aventures de Robinson Crusoë*, made in the 1960s.

Between 1965 and 1968, the U.S. television series *Lost in Space* followed the adventures of the Robinson family, marooned on an unknown planet when their spacecraft is sabotaged. Their attempts to return to Earth are constantly foiled by the villainous Dr. Zachary Smith. The series inspired a movie of the same name in 1998, which featured appearances by most of the cast of the original television series.

ANIMATED FILMS

In *The Castaway* (1931), Mickey Mouse is stranded on a desert island. In *Robinson Crusoe Jr.* (1941), it's Porky Pig's turn to be stranded.

The French series *Robinson Sucroë*, broadcast in the 1990s, features a newspaper reporter who is supposed to write about his experiences on a deserted island. But the island turns out not to be deserted, and Sucroë befriends one of the inhabitants, called Wednesday, who writes the newspaper stories for him.

ROBINSON'S TRAVELS

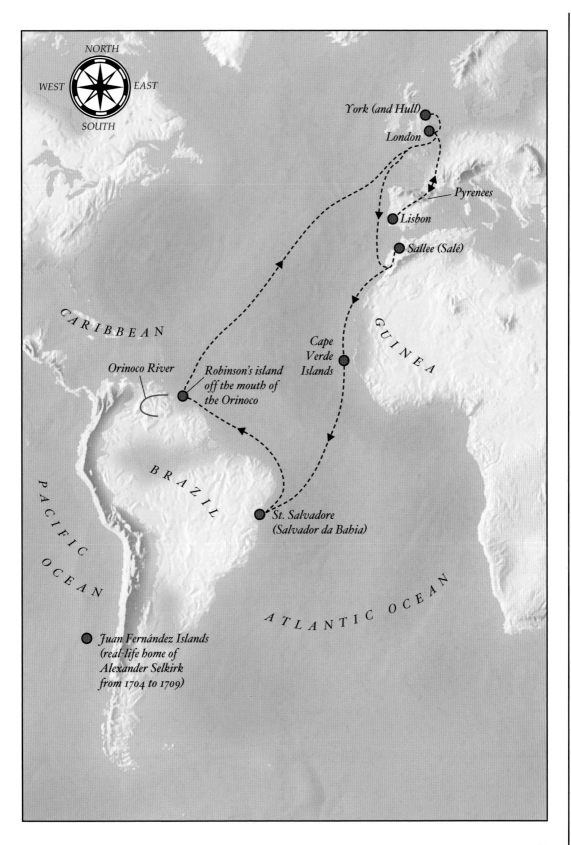

NORTH
WEST — EAST
SOUTH

York (and Hull)

London

Pyrenees

Lisbon

Sallee (Salé)

CARIBBEAN

GUINEA

Cape
Verde
Islands

Orinoco River

Robinson's island
off the mouth of
the Orinoco

BRAZIL

PACIFIC

OCEAN

St. Salvadore
(Salvador da Bahia)

ATLANTIC OCEAN

Juan Fernández Islands
(real-life home of
Alexander Selkirk
from 1704 to 1709)

INDEX

IF YOU ENJOYED THIS BOOK, YOU MIGHT LIKE TO TRY THESE OTHER TITLES IN BARRON'S *GRAPHIC CLASSICS* SERIES:

Adventures of Huckleberry Finn Mark Twain

Beowulf

Dr. Jekyll and Mr. Hyde Robert Louis Stevenson

Dracula Bram Stoker

Frankenstein Mary Shelley

Gulliver's Travels Jonathan Swift

Hamlet William Shakespeare

The Hunchback of Notre Dame Victor Hugo

Jane Eyre Charlotte Brontë

Journey to the Center of the Earth Jules Verne

Julius Caesar William Shakespeare

Kidnapped Robert Louis Stevenson

The Last of the Mohicans James Fenimore Cooper

Macbeth William Shakespeare

The Man in the Iron Mask Alexandre Dumas

The Merchant of Venice William Shakespeare

A Midsummer Night's Dream William Shakespeare

Moby Dick Herman Melville

The Odyssey Homer

Oliver Twist Charles Dickens

Romeo and Juliet William Shakespeare

A Tale of Two Cities Charles Dickens

The Three Musketeers Alexandre Dumas

Treasure Island Robert Louis Stevenson

20,000 Leagues Under the Sea Jules Verne

White Fang Jack London

Wuthering Heights Emily Brontë